Michigan Back Roads
1

by Ron Rademacher

First Edition

Back Roads Publications

6960 Lakeview Dr.

Bellevue, MI 49021

TABLE OF CONTENTS

Michigan Back Roads
1

by Ron Rademacher

Back Roads Publications
6960 Lakeview Dr.
Bellevue, MI 49021

Illustrations – Dawn Baumer – www.dawnscartoons.com

Photographs – Ron Rademacher

Acknowledgments

No book is the work of just one person. This one would not have been written without the unwavering support and excellent proof-reading by Terry Mulvaney and Bruce who knew how to spell Centreville.

Further thanks are due the folks in all of the wonderful small Michigan towns who have made time for my presentations, endless questions and photographic intrusions. Dawn Baumer for her wonderful illustrations. www.dawnscartoons.com

Coming in 2009

Michigan Back Roads – The Festivals

Unique and unusual festivals you might have missed

Michigan Back Roads 2

20 more road trips to special places you might have overlooked.

Michigan Back Roads
1

by Ron Rademacher

Back Roads Publications

6960 Lakeview Dr.

Bellevue, MI 49021

First Edition Volume 1 2009

ISBN 1-57166-549-8

THE APPLE ORCHARD TRIP

The Trip:

There is nothing that says Michigan like fresh apples picked right from the tree. In central Michigan, near Charlotte, is The Country Mill, home of the Michigan Apple Festival. This is an easy drive from almost anywhere in mid-Michigan, has something for everyone and an ever-changing variety of activities depending on the time of year.

What you'll find:

A real working apple orchard farm with thousands of trees. You can pick your own or shop the many varieties in their farm market. The market also has a bakery for fresh apple pie, fresh apple cider and a gift shop.

There is plenty of parking, and it is an easy walk to the orchards. You will find a corn maze, pumpkin patch and a haunted cider mill in the fall. To delight the young kids, be sure to ask about donuts and the fish pond.

Trust me, the children will love it. Spring, summer and fall there is a full day of family fun at The Country Mill.

You can even get married in a special grove in the orchard that has been prepared just for that special purpose.

Directions:

The Country Mill is located in Eaton County. Take I-69 south out of Lansing and take the Potterville exit. The flashing light is Vermontville Highway. Go west about 6 miles and turn north on Otto Rd. If you prefer the back roads, take Rt. 66 north out of Battle Creek or south out of Ionia until you come to the road to Vermontville. When you get to town, continue east onto Vermontville Highway at the "Y" in the road.

Side trips:

Driving through Vermontville is gorgeous in the fall since this is the Maple Valley. If you head south to Bellevue you can try the crab legs at Plezall. This is special, on Saturday from 4:30 p.m. until they run out you can get "all you can eat" crab legs. They bring them out steaming hot on a platter and serve you at your table. When you finish that platter they will bring you another.

A TWO STORY PRIVY

DID YOU KNOW?

TORCH LAKE

IS

CONSIDERED

THE THIRD MOST

BEAUTIFUL LAKE

ON

EARTH?

MICHIGAN'S BRIGADOON

The Trip:

Brigadoon is a legendary town in Scotland that, according to legend, only appears one day every hundred years.

Alden, in northwest Michigan reminded me of this legend the *second* time I visited there. The first time I passed through in the winter and nearly missed the town altogether. If you go in the winter, don't expect much; they kind of close up after Christmas. Spring, summer and fall are a whole different story.

What you'll find:

Alden is the only village that sits directly on Torch Lake. While only a few blocks long, the village is packed with a collection of specialty shops unlike any other town this size that I have ever found. It isn't just the shops, though. Alden's Mill House does produce the best spices in Michigan. There are surprises all around this village, like the Coy Nature Preserve that is a virgin timber area or the historical Museum that has beautiful grounds right on Torch Lake. Torch Lake is considered the third most beautiful lake on earth. On top of that, in keeping with the pace of life here during the warm months, there is a festival nearly every weekend in Alden.

Directions:

Alden is west of Mancelona and north of Kalkaska.

Side trips:

A favorite drive of mine is getting to Alden. If you are coming from the south and go through Kalkaska, head west on 72. About 4 or 5 miles on. you will see a sign announcing the route to Rapid City. This road will also take you to Alden, and the few miles between 72 and Rapid City is

stunning in any season.
Another great side trip is out of Rapid City. Head east at the tavern and travel about 8 miles. On the left will be the 7 Bridges Park, the jewel of Kalkaska county.

Note:

Excellent dining is at hand in Bellaire. Lulu's has made my "Best in Michigan" list; however, the Alden Tavern serves one of the top five burgers in the state and there are regulars there who know where the Morel mushrooms grow.

CLEANEST BEACH IN MICHIGAN

The Trip:

Michigan has more fresh water coastline than any other state. In the lower peninsula, you are never more than 85 miles from one of the great lakes. A trip to the beach is a Michigan favorite and near downtown Muskegon is the cleanest beach in Michigan. It is the only nationally certified "Clean Beach" on the Great Lakes.

What you'll find:

The Pere Marquette Beach on the shores of Lake Michigan and adjoining the Muskegon Lake Channel is the only nationally certified "Clean Beach" on the Great Lakes. Miles of beach, gorgeous sunsets, outdoor dining possibilities, and the newly-complete bike trail make this beach a must-see. Pere Marquette Public Beach and Park covers 27.5 acres and is owned by the City of Muskegon, Michigan. Considered "the best kept secret of Muskegon County," the park contains a number of play areas, sand volleyball courts, and well-kept picnic and sunbathing areas. Pere Marquette Beach offers over 200 feet of paved handicap-accessible walkways to ensure enjoyment for a wide variety of visitors. If you are interested in amazingly beautiful sunsets and walking along uninhabited stretches of sand with your toes in the freshwater surf, Pere Marquette Beach may be the beach for you.

Directions:

From U.S. 31 take the Laketon Ave. exit and head west. Laketon becomes Lakeshore Drive and that will eventually intersect with Beach. The park is the northernmost end of city-owned Lake Michigan frontage that runs for over 2 miles.

Side trips:

The Pier Head Lighthouse is a vintage 53-foot historic structure built in 1851. Take US-31 to Muskegon and Sherman Boulevard. Take Sherman to Beach Street and take Beach Street to the pier.

Downtown Muskegon is rich with history and culture ranging from Victorian-era mansions to the Frauenthal Center for the Performing Arts in the historic Frauenthal Theater.

You can visit three World War II ships including the USS Silversides, a real submarine berthed along the channel wall at Pere Marquette Park adjoining the maritime museum.

Need some local directions? You can't do better than to contact the innkeepers at the Port City Inn Bed & Breakfast.

LAKE MICHIGAN BEACH

A GLOWING TOMBSTONES LEGEND

The Trip:

Midway up the lower peninsula of Michigan is the historic town of Evart. As far back as the late 1800's reports have been made about eerie lights and glowing tombstones in Forest Hill Cemetery. Many have tried to come up with a logical explanation, but none have been successful. Old newspaper reports suggest the phenomenon is caused by the ghost of an Italian railroad worker searching for his son.

What you'll find:

Even if you don't want to mess around in a cemetery after dark, (I did but didn't see the lights.) there is plenty of fun in Evart. The Muskegon River flows through the park, they have music every Saturday night and the historical museum is excellent. Evart is also home to the Dulcimer Festival.

Directions:

Evart is in Osceola County on Route 10 between Reed City and Clare.

Side trips:

Just east of town is Morgan's, the largest producer of organic compost in the Midwest, great stuff for your garden. In town is a park dedicated to Joseph W. Guyton, the first American to die on German soil in WWI and, a favorite for home style cooking, the Corner Cupboard serves it up hot, delicious and plenty of it.

Notes:

A reprint of a 2003 article and the entire history of the railroad and cemetery are on the web site. You can find the "glowing tombstones" legend link in the Evart section of Terrific Towns or there is a link on the Region 4 page on the site.

A HAUNTING IN BARK SHANTY

The Trip:

About halfway up the "thumb" is Port Sanilac, originally known as Bark Shanty. This small village is home to multiple treasures not the least of which is the Loop-Harrison Mansion on the grounds of the Sanilac County Historical Museum. For years there have been tales of encounters in the Mansion. There have been unexplained aromas, voices, apparitions, music and furniture moving about. The locals are sure it must be "Ada". Ada Loop-Harrison had died tragically in front of the Mansion in an auto accident in 1925.

Professional paranormal researchers have established that there is a "presence", most likely benevolent.

What you'll find:

The museum grounds contain several refurbished historic buildings including one of the few operating Barn Theatres in Michigan. The museum grounds are the site of several festivals and events through the year including a top notch wine tasting. The "haunted mansion" is open for tours and can be rented for private functions.

While in town there are a number of art galleries to visit including the Harbor Light Gallery that is inside the Raymond House B & B. This shop contains the works of local artists as well as the wonderful photography by Gary Bobofchak. A nice place to stay if you want to spend the night.

Directions:

Port Sanilac is only an hour or so north of Detroit using I-94 to 25. From eastern Michigan use I-69 to 25 and from Saginaw just take a back road drive on 46 right into town.

Side trips:

A few miles outside of town is the site of the Sanilac Petroglyphs. Revealed by the great fires that swept the region, these are the only known sandstone carvings by native Americans in Michigan. The site also has paths that will lead you through the silent woods for a refreshing walk.

If you want a scenic drive in any season, continue north along the Lake Huron coast on 25. I really like this drive during the winter. Near the tip of the "thumb", you will find Grindstone City and huge grindstones that were manufactured here.

HEMINGWAY COUNTRY

The Trip:

In the northwest section of Michigan are many famous towns and popular destinations. People flock into the Leelanau region little knowing that nearby are several lesser known treasures. Smack in the middle of a triangle marked by Boyne City, Charlevoix and Petosky is a picturesque region known as Hemingway country. Ernest Hemingway was in the region enough for it to make an impression. Today you can still walk the trails that Hemingway walked and see the sites he saw. The cottage of Windemere is still there at Walloon Lake, though it is not open to the public. This region inspired two books, "Up In Michigan" and "Big Two-Hearted River".

What you'll find:

The best way to do this is to get to the village of Horton Bay a few minutes west of Boyne City on C-56. In this small village is the Horton Bay General store for good food and supplies. Next to that is the Red Fox Inn and if you just drive by you are missing a real treat. The owner is a true_ Michigan character and has wonderful books and photos for sale. He has also moved a log cabin and other historic buildings to the property. No one is known to have entered the Red Fox and then left without buying something.

A bit further on is Hortons Creek and it is said that Hemingway did, indeed, catch trout here. A bit further, a small sign at the side of the road indicates the drive to the Horton Creek Inn. You can easily miss this sign; and if you do, you will miss one of the most spectacular and unique bed and breakfast establishments anywhere. The inn is not visible from the road. You have to drive back in and wind through the forest, and then you come out in a clearing where the awesome log lodge appears as if simply lowered down into the 70' tall trees. This may be the most beautiful B & B setting in Michigan in the winter. The snow-laden pines will take your breath away.

Directions:

If you decide to stay in the area for a while, there are a few places I like to visit that you may have missed. The drive around Lake Charlevoix is_ picturesque and beautiful in all four seasons. At one point you will encounter the Ironton Ferry to cross the water. This is a very short ride on a ferry that holds about 3 cars. Great fun but check for winter operation.

If you are in a hurry, it is easy to drive right by the village of Central Lake. If you can find a minute, stop in for some unusual shopping at Adam's Madams downtown. A huge selection with a lot of work by local artists. There is one other very unique shop worth visiting. In East Jordan is a glass-blowing works and the talent there will simply astonish; glass as art that is beautiful and affordable.

Note:

This is the perfect winter getaway if you want to relax and unwind. There is time to just slow down. The Horton Creek Inn B & B is open year around but some of the other locations mentioned close for winter.

One last thing, just my opinion but, The Red Mesa in Boyne City is the best Mexican restaurant in Michigan, period. This is Mexican food like you have never had and it was so good we went two nights in a row even though there are plenty of choices in the region.

Hortons Creek

HIDDEN LAKE GARDENS

The Trip:

In the southeast part of Michigan is a famous region known as the Irish Hills. There are plenty of scenic vistas in the area making it a very popular destination in the summer. On the other hand, there is a spot that is one of our favorite winter day trips. Hidden Lake Gardens is perfect as a "cabin fever" reliever. Just a few miles south of U.S. 12, this one is handy to Detroit or Lansing.

What you'll find:

When you get to Hidden Lake Gardens in the winter you will have a long drive up the winding entrance road to the main buildings. It all looks rather bare in the snow and you may wonder why this is a winter trip. There is the office area where you can shop and get tickets to enter the indoor gardens that are housed in the adjacent domes.

Entering the domes answers all of your questions. The tropical room is filled with palms, flowers and waterfalls. The air is warm, humid and heavily scented by the jungle loam and the flowers that abound.

Nearby is another room that contains an entire southwest desert environment. Warmth again surrounds you but this time it is arid and dry.

There is plenty more but you can discover that for yourself. After even one hour at this wonderful spot you will have forgotten all about the Michigan winter just outside.

Directions:

The garden are located at 6214 Munger Rd. just outside Tipton. Get to the junction of U.S. 12 and 52. Head south on 52 to 50 and go west toward Tipton. Follow the signs. There is also a map link on the website.

Side Trips:

If you go in winter you might want to plan your trip to coincide with the Ice Spectacular in Plymouth. It is regarded as one of the top winter events in America. In summer you can visit the Walker Tavern historic site. For music lovers consider a drive east 30 miles to Hanover, Michigan, and a visit to the Conklin Antique Reed Organ Museum. They have 95 fully restored and working antique reed organs and if your timing is right you can hear them being played. There are other exhibits as well including an 1890's dog-powered treadmill butter churn.

DID YOU KNOW?

THE HIGHEST POINT ON

LAKE MICHIGAN

IS AT THE

OVERLOOK

JUST NORTH

OF

ARCADIA ON M-22.

MICHIGAN HORSE COUNTRY

The Trip:

Forty-five minutes north of Detroit and 90 miles east of Lansing, you can enter a world as far removed from the hustle and bustle of the city as you can imagine. Plan for a full day of pure fun with a surprising variety of things to see and enjoy while doing the whole thing at as leisurely a pace as you desire. Metamora, Michigan, is horse country and is on 24 just south of 69 in Lapeer County.

What you'll find:

A charming Michigan town with artists, very unique shops, cafes and all of it just begs you to stroll the town. Be sure to check out Equine Gatherings. The White Horse Inn, reportedly haunted, offers great food and drink, and at Christmas has horse-drawn sleigh rides around town to view the holiday lights and decorations. If you time it right, you can enjoy their hot air balloon jubilee.

Directions for horse country drive:

You can start with a delightful drive around the horse country. From downtown go east on Dryden until you hit Barber Rd. Go south to Brocker. At this point you can turn west or continue to Rock Valley Rd. and turn west there. Head west to Blood Rd. and go north back to town. It is a gorgeous drive all the way, especially if you love horses.

Side trips:

The Seven Ponds Nature Center is on Caulkins Rd. going south from Dryden Rd. A butterfly garden, glacial lakes and groomed paths make this a favorite for nature lovers.

IARGO SPRINGS

The Trip:

The River Road is a National Scenic Byway that runs along the Au Sable River from Oscoda on Lake Huron west to Route 65. A beautiful drive in any season and along the way is a side road leading to Iargo Springs and the Lumberman's Monument.

What you'll find:

Keep a sharp eye for the turning off the River Road because the signage for Iargo Springs is small. At first you may be puzzled because there is a parking lot and a kiosk with some photos and history but no apparent springs. After you take in the awesome view you will find the stairs to the springs. Be warned, there are 300 stairs and it is a long way down but, for those who make the climb, the reward is like no other in Michigan.

At the bottom of the stairs are the springs. Several are 50 feet across and the water is perfectly clear. There are well-maintained boardwalks that make it easy to wander among the springs. This was considered a sacred place by the natives and it is easy to understand why. Along with the pure water and the views across the wetlands, the only sounds you are likely to hear are the wind in the trees and the cries of eagles. You will not visit a place more magical.

Directions:

The River Road and Iargo Springs are in Iosco County on the Sunrise Side.

Side trips:

The drive along the River Road is wonderful. Just south of Iargo Springs is the Lumbermen's Monument which includes an excellent museum. There are several scenic turnouts along the way. If you continue west on the River Road a few miles, you will come to 65. The drive north to Glennie is a gorgeous winding road of about 20 miles. Also nearby is the Stairway to Heaven, but that will have to wait until the next edition or you can find it on the web site.

WORLDS TALLEST WEATHERVANE

IDLEWILD REVISITED

The Trip:

In Lake County is a town with a unique history that nearly became a ghost town and is now rising again. Idlewild was the first free black community in Michigan. In its heyday it was a premium resort destination with world class entertainment and every amenity imaginable. The town was built by and for African Americans and summers would see a population of 3000+. In the 1920's this town became home for the middle class and a destination for everyone.

What you'll find:

Driving through a year ago was disconcerting. Homes were boarded up and the 60-room hotel on the island was gone, but now there are signs of renewal. A new community center has been built and the museum is open. The signs at the entrance to the community announce that Idlewild may thrive again.

Directions:

Idlewild is on U.S.10 just a bit east of Baldwin.

Side trips:

In nearby Baldwin you can stop for ice cream at Jones Ice Cream and will know you found the best.

The Shrine of the Pines is just south of downtown Baldwin and houses the finest collection of rustic furniture in Michigan.

The Pere Marquette River flows here, world famous for fly fishing for trout.

Pandora's Box is a very cool store in town and a few miles south in Bitely is the Up North Gift Co.

About 10 miles south of Bitely is the Loda Wildflower Sanctuary, one of only a few in America.

Notes:

During the ‘40’s - 60’s Idlewild hosted the biggest names in entertainment like Calloway, Ellington, Armstrong and Hampton. The entertainers were like a “who‘s who“ of the era but there was another man who shouldn‘t be forgotten. Dr. Daniel Williams was a resident and he was also the first to operate on a human heart.

FIELDSTONE BUILDING - LINCOLN

LES CHENEAUX REGION

The Trip:

Here you will find Cedarville and Hessel on the shore of Lake Huron and the gateway to the Les Cheneaux Region. This area boasts unparalleled natural beauty. For hiking, boating or birding this is an area that will call you back again and again. After only a few hours at the shoreline, you will feel all of your cares and worries drift away.

What you'll find:

The area is a treasure trove for nature lovers. Two quaint towns provide all of the amenities while the region preserves its natural beauty in nearly pristine condition. Les Cheneaux means "the channels" and it is these channels between the islands that beckon the kayakers and boaters.

In town are nifty shops, artist galleries and tremendous historical and maritime museums. South of town is a very unique metal sculptor at work. Just follow the signs after the Boat School. The area is also home to the magnificent Antique Boat Show.

My favorite side trips here are all the nature walks and paths you will find at hand. Enjoy the Carl A. Gerstacker nature preserve. (Just try driving around these two towns, and you will discover some of the most beautiful places in Michigan.)

Directions:

After you cross the Mackinac Bridge continue north on I-75 for about 14 miles. Take the exit for route 134 and head east for 17 miles. Plenty of lodging options are at hand, check out Hessel on the Lake.

Side trips:

Of course there is Mackinac Island, but don't overlook Bois Blanc Island as well. This part of the upper peninsula has a dozen lighthouses within a couple of hours. Tahquamenon Falls is less than two hours away. In warm seasons you can climb to the top of nearby Castle Rock to get a view of the islands.

THE SPLIT ROCK

LEXINGTON COLOR TOUR

The Trip:

Not all color tours have to involve a trip hundreds of miles up north. Here is one near Lexington, known as the "First Resort North" and it is in the Thumb.

This tour can start from 1-94 East or I-69 East to Wadhams Road each crosses Gratiot and or Wadhams Road. Take Gratiot North to Wadhams Road about 7.5 miles to Lapeer Road. Turn left (West) at Lapeer Road and go a short distance to

Abbotsford Road and turn right (North)(there are big signs about the Ruby Farms). Abbotsford Road is a winding and turning road through the country.

In less than four miles you will see the Ruby Farm on the left hand side. They have a general store, cider mill and more. They have a huge parking lot so there will be plenty of parking. If you want to all park together, they may be able to rope off an area. After your rest, continue on Abbotsford Road until you reach Avoca Road/136. You will come to a stop sign and turn right and continue East on 136 untill you reach the Dorsey House which will be Wildcat Road. Turn left on Wildcat Road and continue North till you reach M90/Peck Road. There is a stop sign where you will turn right to continue to Lexington. This tour is all blacktop.

What you'll find:

After this short and beautiful drive through the countryside, you will find yourself in Lexington. If you have not visited Lexington before, you are in for a surprise. Downtown is a charming three or four blocks right on Lake Huron, and it is filled with an amazing group of special shops.

Near the lake is a small complex that rivals

anything in the state. A world class theatre, art galleries and fine dining all in one complex. You can easily enjoy an entire day and evening in Lexington.

You will discover that this is a town you want to spend more time in. They have an incredibly effective Arts Council producing several excellent Art Fairs throughout the year and there are a number of Bed & Breakfast establishments to satisfy everyone. The Captain's Quarters is great and men find it quite comfortable. The Primrose Manor may be the most Romantic B & B on the entire Sunrise Side of the state.

Other entertainment:

If you can manage to be in town for breakfast I highly recommend a trip to Wimpy's downtown. Breakfast and lunch are both the kind I like, hot, delicious and plenty of it. In addition to that, listening to the abuse the locals heap on Wimpy and vise versa will have you rolling on the floor laughing.

DID YOU KNOW?

AT LEAST ONE

RESTAURANT

IN

LEXINGTON

IS RUMORED TO BE

HAUNTED?

LONGEST COVERED BRIDGE

The Trip:

The St. Joseph River beautifies parts of south mid-Michigan and provides countless opportunities for enjoying Michigan outdoors. In St. Joseph County you can drive across the longest remaining covered bridge in the state.

What you'll find:

Langley Bridge spans 282 feet across the river. The bridge has three spans, each 94 feet long and was constructed with top quality white pine using the Howe truss system in 1887. It is 16 feet high and 19 feet wide. The bridge had to be raised eight feet when the Sturgis Dam was built in 1910 but still sits very low, almost on the water. One wonders how it has survived floods and river ice.

Directions:

The bridge is about three miles north of Centreville on CR 133. From M-60 turn south on Silver Street west of Mendon.

Side trips:

A day spent riding around this area will produce lots of variety. In nearby Burlington is the Burlington Store. Upstairs is the largest private doll museum in the state with thousands of dolls.

Colon is the "magic capitol of the world".

Lost gold? Back in 1838 in nearby Branch County, Isaac Middaugh heard about a dance and hoedown in the town of Branch. He decided to enjoy himself before continuing his journey but was worried about the quantity of gold he was carrying. Being a prudent fellow he waited until dark so no one would see him and buried his gold along the creek.

Next morning, with a world-class hangover, he went to retrieve his gold. Search as he would, he couldn't find the spot where he buried it, and never did.

Branch is a ghost town now, but if you could find the foundations of the old mill, you might find gold.

THE M-22 DRIVE

The Trip:

A short but sensational scenic drive awaits those who have a little extra time. M-22 runs for about 35 miles along Lake Michigan from Frankfort to just north of Manistee where it intersects with U.S. 31.

What you'll find:

This is a hilly and winding road and some of the most spectacular views of Lake Michigan in the lower peninsula are found along this drive. The turnoff at the CMS Nature Preserve offers a breathtaking scene. Driving south from Frankfort the road begins to climb. You will see two scenic turnouts here and the one on the east side of the road is really worth it. Pull off, get out of your car and look back to the north. All of Frankfort, nestled in its beautiful hills along the Betsie River, will be visible from this spot.

Directions:

From the south or east you can get to M-22 just north of Manistee. The north end of this drive is at Frankfort. There is so much to see and do along this 35 miles that you may want to linger. I can recommend the Arcadia House B&B in Arcadia. The innkeepers know the area well and the Arcadia Historical Museum is at hand as well.

Side trips:

Continue north out of Frankfort on M-22 for just a couple of miles to visit the Betsie Point Lighthouse.

In Frankfort is the Port City Smokehouse. They make the best Lake Trout Pate I have ever had.

The Cabbage Shed in Elberta across Betsie Bay is a good spot for lunch. The food is good and, most importantly, they actually know how to build a Guinness.

The main street in Frankfort ends at the beach, one of the nicest on Lake Michigan. It is well worth the effort to pause here for a sunset. You won't find many any better.

Heading south again you will see a sign for Joyfield Rd. Take that road to Putney Rd. South of the old church is a gravity mystery spot. A map and photo are on the site.

FRANKFORT LIGHT

DID YOU KNOW?

THE GRAVITY MYSTERY

AT

JOYFIELD RD.

IS JUST ONE

OF

SEVERAL

IN

MICHIGAN?

MAGNETIC HEALING SPRING

The Story:

In 1869 some fellows were drilling a well in hopes of tapping into an underground source of brine. They planned to evaporate the water and harvest salt that could be sold. They hit water but it wasn't brine; they claimed it was magnetic. Metal objects dipped in the water, allegedly became magnetic. Not only that, they claimed curative powers for the water as well and within a couple of years St. Louis had become the destination for thousands of folks heading for the baths.

Celebrities came, including General Hooker, Allan Pinkerton and Salmon P. Chase. Documented cures were so numerous that at a time when most roads were mere trails and railroads were scarce, St. Louis got mail 24 times per week. There were churches, libraries, an opera house and first-class accommodations.

Today:

St. Louis is a charming town in the middle of the mitten. The spas and bathhouses are long gone; and the amazing magnetic spring has been capped.

The opera house has been converted, and a drive around town will reveal some extraordinary old homes boasting awesome architecture. St. Louis is worth a stop even if it isn't your final destination. In about one hour and fifteen minutes you can get to St. Louis from Lansing, Saginaw, Bay City, Midland, Houghton Lake and Grand Rapids!

Directions:

St. Louis is on Rte. 46 about an hour north of Lansing. Full details about this amazing chapter in Michigan history are on the site. You can also get the book "The Saratoga of the West" at the Chamber of Commerce.

Side trips:

If you are looking for a beautiful drive, St. Louis is a good place to start. Take Main St. north across the river and turn right on E. Prospect. Go about 3 blocks and turn north again on Union St. As you leave town, this will become Riverside Dr. and will lead you to the Pine River Rd. You can just enjoy the next 20 miles of lovely scenery along the Pine River. This is also a great back road to Midland.

MCCOURTIE PARK (PUBLIC)

The Trip:

In the middle southern Michigan there is a region historically known as the "Irish Hills". Close by major metro areas, this region was and is a favorite for a Sunday drive along U.S. 12, also known as the Great Sauk Trail. Almost directly south of Jackson is Somerset Township and McCourtie Park.

What you'll find:

You won't find anything if you aren't observant; you can easily blow right by this spot and most people do. Keep watch and just east of Somerset Center you will see what appears to be two huge cement trees standing among normal trees on the north side of the road. There is a turning and a small sign announcing McCourtie Park. Take a walk or, better yet, plan a picnic in this unique public park.

The park is several acres and contains a meandering stream. You can cross that stream using any one of seventeen bridges. These bridges are all different. One looks like an old log bridge, and another looks like a suspension bridge. What they have in common is that they are all made of cement and are all the work of one man.

Those concrete trees are actually the chimneys for an underground heating and cooling system for an apartment and garage.

Directions:

McCoutie Park is on U.S. 12 just west of the junction with U.S. 127.

Side trips:

Nearby are the "two towers" that have their own marvelous history. At one time these towers were a major destination for weekend outings.

Hidden Lake Gardens is just a few miles south, one of our favorite winter jaunts. You can go inside and enjoy a southwest desert or a tropical rain forest. What a great break from the winter weather that is right outside!

The Napoleon Café in Napoleon, Michigan can be depended on if you want cooking that is hot, brown and plenty of it.

FIELDSTONE CHIMNEY WORK

OLD VICTORIA (GHOST TOWN)

The Trip:

Thousands of people visit the Porcupine Mountains on the shores of Lake Superior in the western upper peninsula every year; and very few realize that a spectacular drive is nearby that also leads you to Old Victoria. This is a wonderful afternoon day trip from anywhere near the historic town of Ontonagon. Remember that Old Victoria is only open May-September.

What you'll find:

About 18 miles south and east out of Ontonagon is all that is left of an early attempt at copper mining in Michigan. Old Victoria was established around 1771-1772 and judging by the size of the area it was a serious effort. Today you can tour this historic spot and enjoy several structures that have been refurbished by the local historical society. A walk through the cabins and the surrounding area will give you a good idea of how intrepid these early explorers must have been. Everyone talks about the color tours in the U.P. I will tell you that the road from Rockland to Old Victoria will afford some of the most spectacular sights in Michigan in any season.

Directions:

The best way to get there is to leave Ontonagon on 45 and go 12 miles to Rockland. Here you have to turn right on a secondary paved road. There is a sign but it is tiny so it is easy to miss. Not to worry, the Rockland Historical Museum is across the street and they can point out the road.

Side trips:

In case you don't care for ghost towns or are there in the wrong season, here are a few things to check out that are often overlooked. In Ontonagon, the historical museum is great and they have a 3-foot wide chunk of copper from the local mines; the Gitchee Goomie Landing Co. has a couple of very cool shops and they are raising Sturgeon there.

Over in White Pine take time to drive *behind the mall.* You will find the Konteca, a combination Inn and bowling alley. The point is that the dining room has huge windows that are perfect for watching the local bears having lunch. Scruffy is so big that we thought it was a buffalo coming out of the trees.

DID YOU KNOW?

THE SECOND

BIGGEST

ARTS
&
CRAFTS FAIR

IN

MICHIGAN

IS IN

HARRISVILLE?

THE QUILT BLOCK TRAIL

The Trip:

There is nothing like a leisurely drive through the countryside checking out the historic buildings. Up in Alcona County they have added to this by creating a drive to old barns with huge quilt blocks.

What you'll find:

First, you will find a real treasure, Harrisville. This quaint village is right on Lake Huron north of the Au Sable river. Head into the quilt shop downtown for directions and a map. You will take a restful drive through the area viewing huge quilt square replicas mounted on the barns. In addition, another tour is planned to celebrate the 140th Alcona County Anniversary.

Directions:

Harrisville is on Lake Huron at the junction of 72 and 23. If you come in by way of 72, the first quilt block installed is about 2 miles west of town.

Side trips:

There are tons. Sturgeon Point Lighthouse is just north of town and so is the amazing Negwegon State Park. Be sure to visit Moosetales® Gifts for a most unique shop. You can learn more in the unique shops section on the site.

STONE HEAD AT THE MICHIGAN MAGAZINE MUSEUM

WRECK OF THE ELLA ELLENWOOD

The Story:

On an October night in 1901, the schooner Ella Ellenwood ran aground on Fox Point near the Milwaukee, Wisconsin, harbor. Loaded with 150+ tons of wood products, the vessel had left White Lake on schedule but now found itself in trouble. Within a few hours the proud ship was pounded into fragments by Lake Michigan and her northern winds. By the next day there was nothing left.

The next spring a part of the wooden nameplate "ELLENWOOD" was discovered inside White Lake channel. Somehow, the nameplate had drifted across Lake Michigan and found its way into the narrow channel leading to White Lake.

What you'll find:

Montague city hall is where you can see the portion of the nameplate on display. You might want to plan for a full day because Montague and environs is one of the most beautiful areas on the Lake.

The Hart-Montague trail begins here offering hiking, biking and bird watching along the estuary. The Arts Council maintains a gallery of local artists and offers some cool festivals. Plenty of specialty shops and food will make for a great day.

Directions:

Montague and White Lake are located on Lake Michigan near the northern edge of Muskegon County.

Side trips:

The White River Lighthouse is now a museum just south of town and is quite unique with its castle-like structure. Back in town is the wonderful Howmet Playhouse, which offers a full season of top shelf productions.

SECRETS OF CRYSTAL FALLS

The Trip:

Iron County is in the western portion of the upper peninsula; Crystal Falls is the county seat and therein lies one of the secrets. Seems the courthouse was stolen back in the 1800s' after Iron County became a county. The history of this secret is told in full at www.michiganbackroads.com. Another secret is the "falls" themselves. Ask the locals for directions, and they are liable to tell you to go north from the "Split Rock".

What you'll find:

While Crystal Falls is an uncommonly lovely town with spectacular views all around and a remarkable courthouse, it doesn't seem all that unusual. Don't be fooled. You are surrounded with hidden treasures and could probably head for a different destination for a week and not see everything. Here are just a few secrets to discover:

The "Humungus Fungus"

Horse Race Rapids

The River Walk

Winks Woods

Ben Franklin

The Contemporary Center

The Harbour House Museum

The Crystal Theatre

Directions:

Crystal Falls is at the junction of U.S. 2, 141 and 69 about 10 miles north of the Wisconsin border.

Side trips:

In case you need some more to do, try these; Take 69 east for about 30 miles to the town of Felch. Downtown you will find Solberg's, home of the best filet I have found in the U.P. The third cataract of Pier's Gorge is nothing short of breathtaking. There are lots of ways to get there, but this way has some special treats. Take 69 east about 38 miles to Foster City at the junction with G-69. If you go early, you can stop at the Mill Street Inn, a great old U.P. Inn, and have a breakfast of incredible Swedish pancakes and banter with the locals. Head south on G-69 to enjoy the winding road and the Sturgeon river crossings. At U.S. 2 go west to Rte. 8 at Norway. The road to Pier's Gorge is just 7 miles south.

When you are done there, you can head west on U.S. 2 and on the west side of Norway you will see the Norway Spring. Stop there and let the kids find out what real water tastes like. Continue on 2 or take 95 north back to Sagola and Crystal Falls.

Head west about 45 miles to Watersmeet. Go north on Hwy. 45 for about four and half miles to Robbins Pond Road (Old State Hwy. 45). At nightfall you can see the famous Paulding Lights mystery.

Visit www.michiganbackroads.com for even more.

HUMUNGUS FUNGUS?

WHITE PINE VILLAGE

The Trip:

Just outside Ludington, Michigan, you can find the White Pine Village. This is an especially good trip for kids. The village sits on twenty-plus acres and besides lots of activities for children, the grounds provide plenty of room outdoors so the kids can run off some energy in an educational environment. The village depicts life in a small Michigan community of the late 1800's to early 1900's. The village is closed in the winter.

What you'll find:

The village is comprised of 25 buildings, many authentic historic structures, depicting all aspects of Mason County life at the turn of the last century. The self-guided tour will delight the whole family as you wander from building to building. There are thousands of artifacts and displays. Features include: a research library, one room school, log chapel, ice cream parlor, gift shop and old-time baseball. The logwork and chimney work are really special to see.

Directions:

Ludington is on Lake Michigan about an hour and a half north of Grand Rapids. To visit White Pine Village, take Pere Marquette Hwy. south 2 miles from the Mason County Airport, then west on Iris Rd. 1 1/2 miles, then north on 1/2 mile on S. Lakeshore Dr. Note: closed in winter.

Side trips:

Tour the B&B's; there are seven and all are different. The Abbey Lynn Inn is always available for tours and will help you contact the others.

The Carrom Company is in town and have been making games and toys here for decades. Depending on the time of year, you will find fun festivals. One of my favorites is the Sucker Festival in nearby Scottville.

The Jamesport Brewing Company is a very nice micro-brewery, but the Sportsman's is the place to go in this part of Michigan if you are looking for a Rueben sandwich.

TRIP NOTES

TRIP NOTES

TRIP NOTES

TRIP NOTES